For Tilly and Bea
L.B.

To David, Moley and Stripey
G.B.

First published in Great Britain in 2006 by Bloomsbury Publishing Plc,
36 Soho Square, London, W1D 3QY

Text copyright © Louis Baum 2006
Illustrations copyright © Georgie Birkett 2006
The moral rights of the author and illustrator have been asserted

A CIP catalogue record of this book is available from the British Library

ISBN 0 7475 7920 2
9 780747 579205

Printed in China by South China Printing Co.

10 9 8 7 6 5 4 3 2 1

All papers used by Bloomsbury Publishing are natural, recyclable products made from wood grown in well-managed forests.
The manufacturing processes conform to the environmental regulations of the country of origin.

TEA with BEA

Louis Baum   Georgie Birkett

BLOOMSBURY
CHILDREN'S
BOOKS

"Bea is coming to tea today.
Bea's coming to tea with me.
We're going to have fun having tea today."
says Tilly. "Today's the day!"

"When is Bea coming to tea today?
When is Bea coming to tea?"
"Very soon darling, very soon now."
Says Tilly: "Why can't she come
RIGHT AWAY?"

"Why can't Bea come to tea right this minute?
Why can't she come right now

"Let's make a cake for tea," says Mum.

Says Tilly: "Yes, let's make
a cake for Bea,
and let's make it quickly
for tea with Bea."

"Yes, let's make it quickly."
"But gently, gently.
THAT's it," says Mum.

"Let's wash the cups and the saucers and pot, so everything's clean for tea," says Mum.

"Yes, let's," says Tilly, and starts the wash.
"Gently, gently, gently," says Mum.
"THAT'S it."

RING! goes the doorbell.
"Ring. Ring. Whooppee!"
It's time for tea with
Tilly and Bea.

"Hello Bea."

"Hello Tilly."

Says Tilly: "Shall we have a cup of tea?"

"Oh, yes please," says Bea.

"I want to pour the tea," says Tilly.

"No, I want to pour the tea," says Bea.

"No, I want to pour."

"No, I want to pour."

"No, wait," says Tilly. "I know what to do."
"I know what to do as well," says Bea.

Says Tilly: "But I knew what to do first."
"I knew what to do the same time as you," says Bea.

Says Tilly: "So, what should we do?"
Says Bea: "No, you say first."

"No, you say first."
"No, you say first."

"OK. What we should do is have two teapots," says Tilly.
Says Bea: "That's what I think we should do too, but . . .

. . . we've only got one small teeny teapot."
Says Tilly: "Then let's get two BIG ones instead."
"Oh yes, let's get BIG ones. TWO big ones," says Bea.

"Two VERY BIG TEAPOTS for Tilly and me."

"And," says Tilly, "I'll pour it for you."

"And you'll pour it for me," says Bea.

"And," says Tilly, "you'll pour it for me."

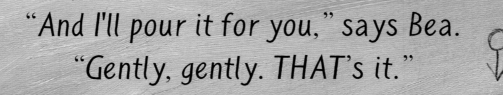

"And I'll pour it for you," says Bea.
"Gently, gently. THAT's it."

Says Tilly: "A lovely cup of tea."

"A lovely cup of tea," says Bea.

Says Tilly: "Another slice of cake?"
"I think I've had more than I should," says Bea.

"Is it time to go?" says Tilly's mum.
"It's long past our bedtime," says Bea's mum.
Says Bea: "Will you come soon to have tea with me?"
"Mmm," says Tilly. "I'd love to come soon to tea."